1   The NUBIAN   (The mysterious NEITH)

« … I captured this idea in passing, and very quickly, I took the first words which came, to express it, lest it flies away . …… »

(Nietzsche)

.

Cover :   ANNA-Maria

2   The NUBIAN   (The mysterious NEITH)

1

Saint - Jean in Lyon. Saturday. Seven in the morning. Pretty month of May. Beautiful sunny morning. On the radio, regular information concerning national news without much importance for a month of May , without particular event except the weather for which the forecast was more optimistic for this beautiful day ahead.

Like every Saturday at this beautiful district of Lyon, the market opened. On the stalls, fresh produce have already started to spread their perfume. Buyers

3   The NUBIAN   (The mysterious NEITH)

sometimes hand in hand, crowd the alleys of this small typical of Lyon market to avoid the rush of the late morning.

That is in this district of Lyon Jimmy lives in an apartment since his divorce, preferring his small apartment, to the beautiful house of his ex-wife located in an upmarket suburb of Lyon.   He feels good even if this apartment is located in this old district in one of the most prestigious parts of Lyon. He was seduced by this district and the beautiful inner courtyards which have retained medieval features and the fact that this area is mainly pedestrian for performing long and pleasant walks.

The decoration of the apartment is more than summary, reflection of his character and his simplicity in his life everyday. He feels at home and can therefore live a life in perfect harmony with his aspirations.

On the same floor in the old building run down, there are three other apartments occupied by neighbors that Jimmy meets very sporadically and with whom he maintains no particular relationship.

Among his neighbors, there is a theater actress, of fourty years, redhead, looking for the role of her life and spending the most of her time to recite verses in front of the mirror of her bedroom, a retired doctor, recent widower, and a slightly worn museum guard, a retired doctor, recent widower, and a museum guard, a bit worn on the bottle, a great lover of military music.

Waking up at seven in the morning is a great luxury for Jimmy because on weekdays, it is usually up and running at five o'clock to go to work in a small silk family company founded ago a hundred years.

Graphic designer, Jimmy took the design manager position in this silk industry and may give free rein to his inspiration while exercising this profession following the centuries old tradition.

After spending more time in his bed while continuing to listen to the alarm clock radio, Jimmy decided to get up. No purpose in his head, nothing special to start this morning. The day promised to be beautiful and radiant : an early morning walk was needed to breathe

6   The NUBIAN   (The mysterious NEITH)

and to enjoy this rare moment.

Returning to the kitchen where he had lighted up the coffee maker, Jimmy went now, into his small bathroom of which is his pride. The apartment had been inhabited by a painter who has painted a pastel blue fresco on the tiled wall above the tub, giving the impression of a larger space and allowing a reverie, an escape during this special time of the bath.

It must be said that in Lyon, the mural is a real tradition, the most famous being the fresco called " The Lyonnais" totaling twenty five historical characters of Lyon, and six contemporary figures on the bottom of the fresco.

On the way to the bathroom, his

approach is nonchalant, dragging his slippers, as to mark that time which belongs to him, in this fine morning. It almost sacred moment, and which does not bode important and urgent affair , in an immediate future.

2

After a hearty   breakfast completed with a fruit salad, Jimmy went to his bedroom. He wears a jeans trousers, a white shirt with sleeves and a blue sky sweater, tied around his neck.

Having finished tying the laces of his blue colored shoes , Jimmy rushed out of the apartment located on the second floor. He borrowed the stairs like an athlete, and gushes in the street outside the building, happy to enjoy this radiant morning.

Following his instinct, he is heading now to suit his mood through those streets already invaded by all sorts of people going about their business. He crosses tourist groups whose program of the day included a prerequisite tour in this picturesque district of Lyon. His ears can catch up all kinds of languages, but it does not care about this invasion in his beloved neighborhood.

From time to time Jimmy was accustomed to do his market on Saturday morning, but that day, the program was different : wander here and there. So, from street to street, from place to place during this frantic wandering , (such a bee in summer blooms, flitting from flower to flower), as if it was the first time he discovered this neighborhood. His exhilaration was palpable: nothing could taint or thwart his good humor. It was beautiful to see. Is because of the effect of the sunlight that flooded the old city of Lyon for their warmth after a particularly cold winter, or simply, was he happy to be alive, happy to live, happy to get the chance to enjoy life and this exceptionally nice time?!

For him, he had to be there , in this moment (for sure!). Nothing else.
Suddenly, without knowing why, his steps had led him into the shop of this very old bookseller. He stopped as if he was automatically guided . A moment later he mechanically entered into the shop.

Behind the counter, the old bookseller does not pay attention to anyone. He is immersed in reading a few books, taking advantage of the opportunity to be the custodian of this ancient knowledge.

How can we become bookstall by definition, if we do not like this hidden knowledge, or if we do not known how to flush this ancient knowledge through those old books which have no price but which are sold with a low price (because they are old) to allow to the amateurs we are, to enjoy this ancient knowledge without much expense?

Can the knowledge be obsolete? This is another debate.

Jimmy is rather fond of comics . That is this passion that led him to undertake graphic studies. But in comics as in many areas, there are many candidates and few chosen. Hence his conversion in the design applied to the silk.

But then, What is he doing in this old shop books usually dedicated to some austere treatises ? Had he a clear idea in his head, which irresistibly and more or less unconsciously pushed him to this shop?

Always obedient to this strange force, he stopped in front of a shelf containing several ancient books. Among these old books, his attention is drawn to a very old photo album . He grabbed the photo album, opened it and realized that he was a virgin album. He turned it, to allow him to see the sales price and read : "5 euros". He hesitated a moment, then puts his hand into his pocket and walked to the cashier.

After this purchase very unusual, unexplained frenzy that inspired Jimmy disappeared as if by magic. He immediately returned at home and he did not know why. He took the stairs (four at a time) to get into the apartment. Once inside his apartment, at first, he put this album (still wrapped in its old original wrapping paper) on his coffee table in the middle of his living room, then went to the kitchen to take a glass of brandy. He return back to the living room and took a seat in front of the table, strangely fixing this object he had just acquired in the bookseller shop.

The last photos album he had had in his hands was one that contained pictures of his daughter Sylvia he had with his wife native of Lyon Floriane, with who he was divorced for about two years.

Floriane, only daughter of a rich industrialist from Lyon, was married with Jimmy after a tumultuous divorce and after scouring the warm waters of the Caribbean to allow her to forget her first husband with whom , she had no children. She needed someone like Jimmy, not only to fill her loneliness, but also because of the discret character , ideal character to perfectly dominate him, as Floriane is the dominant genre, a little "daddy's girl", a little "spoiled child", or all that at the same time. Jimmy was aware of this fact but this had not prevented him from falling madly in love with this charming and delightful person. From this union was born Sylvia, now aged ten years.

Floriane had consented to Jimmy to take and to keep the family album, album in which pictures of their daughter are the most numerous and recalling some essential point in their married life. And this "family" album

was already prominently in his library.
So why this new album?

3

Jimmy spent the rest of the morning to clean his apartment, using the vacuum cleaner in all rooms and putting everything in order as usual each weekend. He prepared the laundry bag for laundry and rested a moment while continuing to question about his acquisition made a few hours earlier.

After lunch with the remains of a meal bought the day before at a caterer, he answered to two or three letters, filled some checks to pay outstanding invoices, gave a phone call to his daughter to have fresh news of his small family. The news seems reassuring to that side. Nothing important: his daughter is doing well and is preparing with great excitement her next birthday party with her girlfriends. Always equal to herself Floriane told him her new troubles with her new hairdresser. She feels awfull with her new hairstyle and does not know where to turn to find the rare pearl likely to cut her hair as she would have wished. Jimmy listened to all this with half an ear, simply by occasionally responding   " Oh really? ".

The old album always sat in the same place.

The day was uneventful, without new impulses , without new questions. The "thing" seemed like black cohosh, as if it was undeniably the beginning of a great event in becoming , and of which the first element , just took place..

Yet Jimmy does not have this propensity to pollute the mind with this type of consideration in connection with a predisposition to have premonitory intuitions or concerning a fact likely to augur an extraordinary event.

The truth is that Jimmy is a disconcerting and rational person. For him everything can be explained and as he spent part of his life to fight against Floriane who is a follower of spiritualism. Some evenings, their home strongly resembled to the salons of clairvoyance with all that that could carry as whiff of the afterlife. Jimmy hated those evenings when he had no place in his own house, even if its origins could influence a possible adherence to theses defended by his beloved wife Floriane. His only way out was to be alone with his daughter upstairs.

Jimmy is from one of the big three traditional groups of Pacific Ocean islands, namely Melanesia (black islands) to the east and north of Australia.

Solomon Islands are his homeland, Jimmy has kept the sense and respect for traditions. Going to the Seaside, to have connections with the Sea, are attitudes from another time but needed to invoke and maintain contact with the protective spirits of his people.

Based in Honiara (Solomon Islands capital, located on Guadalcanal Island), Jimmy's family had prospered thanks to the deep sea fishery industry, created by the grandfather John fifty years before the birth of Jimmy, whose activities were extended to all islands Choiseul, New Georgia, Santa Isabel, Malaita and Makira.

Due to its success, the fishery industry has allowed the entire family to gain some respectability in the Solomon Islands community , and to send Jimmy to study in Europe.

4

The encounter of Floriane and Jimmy had occurred in Malta in a scuba diving group. Due to his origins, Jimmy is a great scuba diving enthusiast. On his island, he used to practice this sport without diving equipment.

For its part, Floriane was initiated by her first husband who had grown up in the West Indies. Both thus had the passion of the sea.

Because of this closeness with the sea, a spiritualist mage that Floriane frequented assiduously, had "decreed" that she had been created by a powerful spirit of the sea, and only a person "authorized" by the powerful spirit of the sea, could especially be her husband and could stay her husband .

In short, it was to meet the wishes of this cosmic begetter, demanding and merciless. And of course from the point of view of the Honourable spiritualist mage, the "approved" husband would be someone who would not object to the organization weekly meetings during which, Floriane must put a lot of bank notes on the table.

Deeply and irreparably marked by this "revelation", Floriane had left herself gradually be overwhelmed by the idea of the need to find the "real man" for her , coming from the ocean depths like herself, and this man would immediately be recognized by her spiritualist mage.

From that moment, Jimmy could not

fight against the grip on his wife. Otherwise, nothing was wrong between them, at the contrary. The first years of their union were more than happy. Floriane was really in love with this boy come from islands, tall , strong, bronze color eyes, cultivated, with a strong sense of family chief responsibility, a little at a Solomonic way.

The Solomonic tradition was integral to the life of Jimmy. But it was obvious that it could not be applied in the state, to this good old earth of Lyon. While it is true that the majority of the Solomon Islands population is Christian and 99%, Christianity has had a profound influence, even if social structures and traditional customs are still very important and perennials. At all times, the Solomon Islands have lived very grouped within their family groups, linked by common standards and obligations, not by individual expectations, but by encouraging practices to care for others and to help each other ensuring shelter, food, clothing, money and work. Moreover, family ties are very strong: the extended family takes care of the young, the sick and the elderly. Children move freely within the family group. The social network guarantee perfect security protecting children and the majority of the population against poverty.

This difference in cultures was palpable in their couple. During the many discussions that animated from time to time their rare evenings (without the spiritualist mage), this significant difference in their cultures, regularly was in addition of a difference of opinion on how to educate their only daughter, education based on the core values governing how to behave at all times, face to adversity in particular.

For Floriane, the courage is the sacred value while for Jimmy, the solidarity is the key word. Great adept of philosophy, Floriane never failed to remind his Platonic view on the need either to assume our fear of an objective risk or considered dangerous in an exceptional situation, ie the obligation to take into account the Courage when the we must face the sad everydayness of the life, emotionally, physically or professionally. For her, it is in this light that they must raise their daughter to prepare her for the world of tomorrow, convinced herself of the difficulty of being on this earth as she used to say, despite his golden childhood.

For Jimmy, Marcus Aurelius was right when he wrote:

« *All beings are bound by a sacred knot.* ».

This phrase sums up his understanding of the concept of solidarity, solidarity between men being essentially a cosmic reality. This belief allows him to fight the idea of "everyone for themselves".

5

Monday morning. Jimmy went to work as usual. Like every Monday, summit meeting to discuss current projects and to take into account the new orders.

Jimmy has the opportunity to work at this time on the project from a rich family of the Arab - Persian gulf, forcing him to rethink the traditional technique of silk workers. The extravagance of the rich clients, ignores traditional techniques in force and thousands of hours of work that will be necessary for completion of the project "Pharaonic" at the scale of small business in which Jimmy works .

Despite this workload, Jimmy's spirit turns from time to time towards this album remained at the same place on the table.

In his imagination of rational being (as for all the common men) , a photo album is used to store pictures. But aside from that role "ordinary" vested in an 'ordinary' object, Jimmy gradually sees another possibility to explain the arrival of this album from the bookshop to his home.

The weight of the basic function of this album did not seem to correspond to the service he could expect. It would be too banal to think that an album, only could store pictures. Jimmy does not want and can not be satisfied with this simplistic view of this unusual object that is this album. Then his imagination began to run very fast.

Quick lunch break in the district of his company. On the way back, Jimmy made a detour to the Republic Street (formerly Imperial Street) without knowing why. He rushed into a big high tech store and decided to buy a modern and sophisticated camera.

With this purchase, Jimmy seemed once more, to have obeyed to another pulsion, maybe the same as last Saturday. Who knows ? Is this a second stage of the same event in preparation? An old album, a camera : what else to complete what could unhesitatingly be called the Jimmy's puzle event ?

Back home at the end of his work day, Jimmy did some shooting tests from his window on the second floor of the building and began to play the perfect photographer. This pleasure lasted only a moment. He put the device in its holster, placed it alongside the album and went about his business.

On the assumption that Jimmy has completed these purchases without giving special meaning to his behavior, it remains that this is a phenomenon that completely escapes him through this implementation of unconscious actions process.

Seen from the exterior, why these "micro events" constitute they a problem? Without necessarily seeking to unravel the mystery surrounding these purchases, mystery defining these instinctual behaviors demonstrated by Jimmy so far, it may only be that the result of an unconscious thought to establish or implement an event which nobody, at this time, can predict the end.

6

One day during his lunch break, while walking in a shopping mall in La Part-Dieu district , Jimmy's attention was caught by a small poster on which a female person offered to pose for a photographer or a painter. He stopped in front of this poster. He read and reread it as if he did not understand the meaning of this announcement was quite simple and clear.

On the other hand, being neither painter nor photographer, how could this announcement represent any interest for him? After a moment of hesitation, he detached one of the precut sheets mentioning the telephone number of the young person, then he carefully put

it into his pocket and continued his tour
through the gallery.

Since his visit to the mall, Jimmy had
not thought about this sheet until the
following Saturday when preparing the
laundry bag for laundry. When
checking the pockets of his shirts
before putting them in the bag, he
discovered the famous sheet and
remembered suddenly that poster. He
sits on the edge of the bathtub,
unfolded the sheet and read it over the
phone details. No name, no last name,
just the phone number. He dropped
what he was doing, got up and ran to
the living room. He grabbed the mobile
phone and dialed the number on the
sheet.

Heart pounding, he heard a first ring
followed by a second and suddenly he

interrupted the communication before the call succeeds. He had just realized that he was neither a painter nor photographer. Yet the desire to talk with that person was stronger than him, as pushed by a new impulse, he recomposed the number.

After several rings, response to the other end.

   The unknown : « *Allo* »
   Jimmy : « *Hello, I call you about your ad.*»
   The unknown : « *Oh Yes, but I have already received several proposals* »
   Jimmy : « *Oh really ?... * »
   The unknown : « *Several weeks ago, I put that ad. I normally working for the architecture school, replacing someone who was on maternity leave.*

She returned from her leave and I needed to find something to allow me to earn my money ....»

Jimmy : *«OK, So you have everything you need? »*

The unknown : *« Normally yes, but may I ask what you are doing in this area? »*

Jimmy : *« I am neither a photographer nor a painter. But make no mistake about me. I'm not trying to find a babysitter. I do not have a baby. I just want to participate in a competition and I need to make a photos book. Do you understand me ?»*

The unknown : *« A photos book ? As for the models? »*

Jimmy : *« Not exactly a manikin will present through a series of photos the extent of her modeling talent, while I have to show I can do pictures.»*

The unknown : *« And what kind of pictures have you to do ? »*

Jimmy : *« I do not know. That is a free subject and this is the first time, I participate to such a competition. You have an idea of what we could do as the type of pictures if you were free?»*

The unknown : *« It belongs to you   to say ... .. I hope you are not doing me a bad joke!»*

Jimmy : *« Not at all ! »*

Jimmy knew he was not telling the truth to the person who looks rather perplexed, face to this guy who introduced himself as a future participating in a photography contest.

Jimmy was in a complete improvisation without knowing where that would lead him. This puts him uncomfortable, but still appearing   to be within the scope of this impulse that never left him until now, he tried the all out..

Jimmy : « *Would you like us to do better acquaintance with a drink tonight or tomorrow if you're free?* »
The unknown : « *you really think this is necessary?* »
Jimmy : « *Yes ! Please, say yes!* »

No sound from the other side of the line.

Jimmy : «Are you still there*?* »
The unknown : « *Yes I do* »
Jimmy : « *Then ?* »
The unknown : « *The problem is that ,I do not know what to tell my boyfriend. He knows that my diary is full* »

Jimmy felt that the affair is escaping to him and he cannot resolve to let it go.

Jimmy : « *Ok ok ! I give you my address and I hope to hear from you soon* »

Jimmy did note his phone number and full address. The stranger thanked him and ended the call.

7

Several weeks have passed since the phone call totally improvised. Life seemed quietly run its course in the small apartment in the old building. The old / new album and the new camera are always in the same place in the living room on the table.

Meanwhile, the highly anticipated and very coveted birthday party of Miss Sylvia took place in the presence of her maternal grandparents, of many girlfriends and of course the spiritualist mage whose only with his presence , he could give the guarantee of a successful party, to the despair of Jimmy.

It was an opportunity for Floriane and

Jimmy to meet again. The latest news Floriane is that , she still is searching for her "cosmic husband" , actively assisted by the Right Honourable spiritualist mage.

One night around 8pm , somebody rings the doorbell. Jimmy who does almost never get a visit, wonders who it could be at this hour of the evening.
It was hot. Jimmy, wearing a simple summer clothes, got up and walked to the door and asked:

« Who is there ? »

A female voice behind the door answered:

« Neith »

Jimmy who does not know anyone in Lyon responding to that name, remained speechless for a while , then :

« What do you want from me ? »

The voice behind the door :

« I am the person you contacted for the photo contest. Am I bothering you ? »

Jimmy : *« A moment, please. »*

Jimmy rushed into the bedroom to dress more appropriately, then came back to open the door.

Neith *(smiling) : « Good evening, do I disturb you? »*

Jimmy could not believe it : by opening the door, he found the most beautiful creature that it was ever given to him to see. He had before him a Nubian lady. An indefinable color resulting from a splendid mixing Egyptian - Sudanese, an oval face, thin nose, mouth very discreet, light brown eyes , long hair, black ebony. svelte look, discreet breast size in the upper middle.

Neith is wearing white trousers, a top color azure and a pair of ballerinas red blood . Her face is smiling and extraordinarily radiant.

In ancient Egypt, her name means "Divine Mother." Name she inherited from her grandmother, a very religious person who wanted that she dedicated herself also to religious occupations.

43   The NUBIAN   (The mysterious NEITH)

But, Neith decided otherwise, by studying during years, classic letters , within the Faculty of Arts and linguistics of Besançon in France. And then one day, she met a fellow who asked her to follow him in Lyon, city which he extolled the charms constantly, until she has accepted to follow him to live there in Lyon. They have been together just for a short period. The fellow also liked the charms of beautiful ladies of Lyon and Neith does not like to share.

Neith had no other recourse than to seek the means to earn a dignified life. Taking the pose for painters or photographers, is not a natural attitude for her, for her own nature imbued with a certain modesty, but also because of the strict upbringing she received from her grandmother who had raised her after her mother died when she was ten years.

> **Jimmy** : « *Do not stand at the door, I beg you, come in!* »
> **Neith** : « *Thanks* »

Neith entered into the apartment, hesitantly, a little bit embarrassed to have made this impromptu visit. This way of acting is her nature : spontaneous, a little daredevil but extremely lucid. Jimmy closed the door behind her.

> **Jimmy** : « *Take a seat , please*»

Neith accepted and sat on the sofa. Jimmy sat facing her in one of the armchairs.

Jimmy : « *Coffee ?*»
Neith : « *Do you have something stronger? I fear I can not sleep if I take a coffee at this hour.*»
Jimmy : « *Whisky ? Brandy ?* »
Neith : « *Brandy please* »

Jjimmy disappeared for awhile in the kitchen and comes back with the brandy bottle, two glasses and did the service , a little shaky while imagining the coming events..

Jimmy : « *Cheers !* »
Neith : « *Cheers !* »

Ordinary brandy. First sips. No reaction from Neith. Jimmy tries to adopt a natural posture, crossing and uncrossing his legs. Neith observes all this, her glass , enclosed in the palms of her hands, and calmly sipping her brandy, as to give herself courage.

> **Neith** :«*So tell me what is this contest?* »

Jimmy feels trapped but tries a diversion :

> **«And your boyfriend? ...** ***You could free yourself?*** »

> **Neith** : « Yes »
> **Neith** : « Then*?* »

Neith is waiting for his answer, urgently.

> **Jimmy** : « *... I wanted to participate to this contest. ....* »
> **Neith** : « *And you don't*

want anymore? »

   __Jimmy__ : « ... but seeing you I thought that ... »

   __Neith__ : « I do not fit what you were looking for? »

Faced to this flood of scathing replicas at each of his response attempts, Jimmy does not know where to turn. Replicas of Neith contrasted sharply with the apparent softness of her beautiful face.

   __Neith__ : « There is no contest, is not it? » she said calmly.

Even before Jimmy answers to that ultimate question, Neith seized the brandy bottle and filled her glass. A good dose. Jimmy did the same thing. Losing the face with a glass of brandy in his hand will be something

© *Nathanaël AMAH , 2016* *NATHAM Collection*

honorable . Surely an old adage Solomon!

Suddenly :

> **Neith** : «   Can you make me visit your apartment and maybe your photo studio? »

Jimmy feels lost.

> **Jimmy** : « OK ! »

Neith stood up, still the glass of brandy in her hands, ready to make the tour of the apartment. Jimmy did not have other choice than to get up in his turn to guide ahead of what for him will be the supreme humiliation of his life, him who always controls events in his life and around of his life.

The brandy helping him , Jimmy takes the initiative and leads the way in head towards the kitchen. Neith follows him like his shadow, and sticks his head through the door to discover the kitchen, functional but tiny. Back in the living room.

Jimmy : « *Living room* »

Neith smiles.

Neith : « *This, I already know ! »*

Jimmy does not let himself overwhelmed

« ***Yes, but original wooden floor! please !!!!!***»

Neith smiles again. Jimmy

continues the visit, opening the toilet door.

Jimmy : « *Toilet bowl , not original. I am sorry.* »

This time Neith laughs. The tour continues. Suddenly, Jimmy had the bright idea to head to the bathroom and said with a clear voice by opening the door of the bathroom :

«*My studio! Here is my studio!*»

Neith discovers with great surprise this wonderful and unexpected fresco above the bathtub. She remains speechless for a moment then :

«*I should take a bath , then?* »

At his turn to smile.

> ***Jimmy*** *: « yes to some extent. .... Since the moment I hear to talk about sirens, I can finally take a pic of a real mermaid. This will be the theme of my photos, of course if you still agree to consider my proposal. »*
> ***Neith*** *: « So you mean that there really is a photo contest? »*

Jimmy does not answer the question and continues the visit.

> ***Jimmy*** *: « My bedroom »*

Neith enters the room. She takes a few steps and returns back the question again :

« *There really is a photo contest?* »

Jimmy enters in his turn in the room, his glass of brandy in hand. He sits at the foot of his bed, Neith is stand , facing him against the wall.

> ***Jimmy*** : « *.... You see, it's a long story. I'll try to explain. ...* »

For several minutes (the brandy having finally and completely uninhibited him), Jimmy told a high level tale, trying to explain somehow why he had contacted her.

Neith very stoically listened to him, then leaves him.

9

Neith has gone into the night as she had come. Jimmy closed the door and returned to the living room. A cognac steam mixed with the smell of Neith's fragrance fills the air. Jimmy opened the window to ventilate. Was he dreaming? What had he told Neith? What he has promised?

Not able to realize what had happened, Jimmy slid into the sofa. This is no longer the same man from before the surprise visit of Neith. Facing him on the table, still these two strange objects that compose the old / new album , and the new camera. Both objects suddenly got a special significance following this visit, which seems to fit of the same logic as the previous events, which competed the "mysterious" and unexpected purchase of a photo album and a camera .

Suddenly the phone rang, rooting out him from his torpor.

Jimmy : « *Allo* »

No answer. Jimmy can hardly guess a breathing breath in his handset.

Jimmy : « *Allo !* »

On the other end after a few seconds of silence and then :

« It's me ...... the siren! .... That's true what you told me? »

Above all, for Jimmy, it was absolutely necessary to recover his clouded minds and imperative to remember what was said in the bedroom there is barely an hour. How to remember what was said then that he absolutely can not do it to the extent that it was undeniably like in a daze during this part of the evening he had spent with Neith! Not because of the brandy, but because this whole story seems to be based on nothing, although the events seem to contradict this thesis.

Answering to this question that Neith has asked , is not within only of his understanding. It seems that during those long minutes that he took to expose and explain his fake project to Neith, he was in action as an actor, all fully focused on the need to convince Neith to take part in this mysterious project. In the bedroom, he was in the shoes of a person responding to a stimulus of which he had no conscience, of which he ignores the scope, significance and consequences regarding to his statements. Jimmy is as if struck by a sudden amnesia, as if all he had said in his bedroom, had not been said by him.

This simple question that requires a simple answer becomes very complicated for him. The perfect legitimacy of this question, however, may bring Jimmy to a certain reality as if since her home, Neith is in the process of looking at his eyes to make sure whether she can trust him.

Jimmy : « Sure *!* »

There is a natural instinct in Neith : both curious, but not too much, skeptical but just right what is necessary, suspicious if her instinct commands her to be prudent.

In this "game" in which she had to engage with a partner,(someone she just met and of whom she knows nothing), she can not determine.

Paradoxically, shefeels captive of this "partnership" : she feels neither suspicious, nor confident. A kind of neutrality or even a complete lack of will. Nothing can tilt her to one side or the other. Indeed, what more easy for her to decline the offer? Instead, here she is rushing into the unknown. She probably wants to express a form of freedom of thought, absolute freedom in her attitude and her action. Intuitively, the "voice" of the unknown towards who she is willing and ready to head herself , may be very similar to the voice of destiny because in this case, she seems to take refuge in what she ignores.

Neith : « *What's that siren story?* »

The mystery deepens. Why now, she speaks of mermaid? Oh yes, Jimmy remembers his words in the bathroom and his allusion to the siren. However, by seriously thinking about it , the evocation of this siren is not related to the forthcoming sessions of shots of aquatic photos, but to his painful past between Floriane and spiritualist mage.

"Officially," according to the conclusions of the very serious study made by the no less honorable spiritualist mage about Floriane, she would be a kind of siren as generated by a powerful spirit came from the seabed. Allegations to which, Floriane has perfectly and totally adhered and which had been the starting point of the separation and the divorce of the couple.

10

Called Youssoufou,   the spiritualist
mage is from a country of East Africa,
who fled his country in war and
installed since   many years in this
region of Lyon, and has thrived with
his spiritualist activities.

He enjoyed a major reputation in this
environment where, idleness (corollary
of a certain richness) makes the people
he approached, totally receptive to his
allegations, forecasts or judgments.

Many of his "Friends" have made his
fortune. As a result, he had built in the
exclusive suburb of Lyon, a beautiful
lodge where his three wives (come
from Africa) and their several children,
live a quiet life thanks to flourishing
"trade" of the master, without fears at

the nose of french authorities, in a country where polygamy is prohibited.

The trade of Youssoufou is invariably based on his "ability" to reconnect the spirits of the sea to the poor souls who do not have the awareness or knowledge of their "line" with the said spirits of the sea, line through which the concerned people (preferably already very rich) have acquired their fortune, straight come from the seabed, (according to the very respectable mage), fortune generously backed by the powerful sea spirits (male and female) and which are waiting in back consideration and recognition towards them. His role is to propose himself, as the indispensable friend and intermediary, depository of customs in force in the seabed to approach and consult these powerful spirits of the sea towards which he has to visit in the summer time , from time to time, either in Deauville or in Cannes (or in other prestigious seaside places in France) with all the expenses paid and with comfortable financial means for offerings to please the spirits. It surely was necessary to go into these prestigious places to establish contact with his famous "sea interlocutors".

For the case "Floriane", the conclusions of the mage were clear : Floriane is a siren of the lineage of the goddess of the seas. Jimmy knows only too well the devastation that these allegations had produced on his ex wife.

Since then, for him, the word "mermaid" has a meaning and a

particular taste.

Jimmy : « I do not know what I have say to you about mermaid, but know that I lived with a mermaid in another life. »

Neith : « Oh really ? »

Jimmy : « Yes Please, let's stop talking about all this.»

Neith : « Ok ! ..... When could we meet , I mean for photos?»

Jimmy : « You really want? »

Neith : « Sure ! But I can only come at night. »

Jimmy : « And what about your boyfriend? I thought that... »

Before ending talking Jimmy is

interrupted curtly :

> *« I do not have a boyfriend.. . At least not right now. »*
>
> ***Jimmy*** *: « OK ! Next week ? I have to take some days off , and I can devote time to the preparation of sessions »*
>
> ***Neith*** *: « Perfect ! Bye. »*

End call.

To end this eventful evening, Neith took a hot bath before going to bed.

She has not understood everything. But she is well aware that nothing seemed "normal" in this affair. However, she did not want to protect herself. She wants to participate in these sessions pictures. She wants to do this experiment without knowing why. In a role of siren in a bathtub or lying in front of the students of Arts schools, for her, until this moment, it makes no difference even if the data do not meet the criteria usually considered to accept and honor a contract of this type.

This meeting with Jimmy had made her somewhat nervous and she could not sleep . She picked up again the handset from the phone and recomposed Jimmy's number.

Same situation with Jimmy, still sitting on his sofa, finishing his brandy .

Jimmy : « *Allo* ».

Neith, from her bed :

« *It's me again. Am I*

bothering you? »

Jimmy : « No, I'm not *sleeping.* »

Neith : « I cannot sleep .. »

Jimmy: «What should be done? Want a lullaby? »

Neith : « ...Do you want to come see where I'm living? »

Jimmy : « Now? »

Neith : « Yes, I would love. »

Jimmy, increasingly perplexed in front of this last twist of fate, but after a few seconds of hesitation:

« ...It would not be reasonable .... We work tomorrow , you do not remember? »

Neith : « You will stay just 5 minutes. Say Yes ! Please ! »

Jimmy looks at his watch: : 11pm.

> *« It is late, it really would not be reasonable. Let's put it in tomorrow if you wish.»*
> **Neith** : *«You will stay only 5 minutes»*

Jimmy does not know what to do. Will he take the risk of displeasing Neith that he struggled to convince? Does he really have the ability to decide anything in this matter? The situation seems to escape him completely again. He takes one last look at his watch:

> *« OK, 5 minutes »*
> **Neith** : *« Great, I'm waiting for you »*

11

Jimmy jumps into a taxi. Nestled at the back of the taxi, Jimmy can not believe what he is doing. In his ears still reasons Neith's voice: "I'm waiting for you." Particular voice letting appear a certain coldness, a perfectly mastered speech, neither too fast nor too slow but expressing things with calm and determination.

The taxi has left the old Lyon towards BELLECOUR. Jimmy still is in his thoughts. He can not make sense of this event which began strangely and who is now continuing the same way. GUILLOTIERE - The taxi continues its path, leading Jimmy to Neith. - SAXE GAMBETTA - Dense traffic. The taxi slows down. Jimmy threw a last glance at his watch. Almost midnight. - LAENNEC - The taxi marks a stop at the red light, in front of the medical school. Neith is not far away. Home stretch. Jimmy begins to feel bad. Finally VENISSIEUX at the address indicated.

Jimmy pays the note and exits out of the cab. Front of the building, he marks a pause before engaging in the lobby. Light pressure on the intercom button.. Seconds later, a click, and the door opens . Jimmy goes now to the elevator that took some time to arrive. Last chance for him to return at home. But pushed by this force that he still can not control, he pressed the button N° 8. The door of the elevator closes. Starting the wheezy old elevator. The lift laboriously led him to the 8th floor. No speed record. When exited out of the elevator, Jimmy discovers four apartment doors on the landing. A door is ajar revealing a glimmer in the apartment. On hesitating, Jimmy goes to the door and looks inside.

«Neith! It's me .... Jimmy ... Here I am! ... We have said 5 minutes is not it ? »

As out of nowhere, Neith appeared before Jimmy and invited him to enter before closing the door behind him.

It was no longer the same person. She seemed modern in her spring outfit, worn early in the evening, is transformed now into an oriental woman wearing a kind of pale pink sari , hair flowing over her shoulders, eyes cleansed, but the painted lips of bright red.

The fragrance worn by Neith was not at all the same as in the early evening. Strangely, Jimmy seems to know this fragrance.

Since the arrival and the reception of Jimmy, Neith has not loosened teeth, just contenting herself to smile as to express some satisfaction to have him there, in front of her at this late hour of the night.

Neith hands him a glass with plum and added :

> « *Do you want to eat something?* »

Jimmy smiled and replied :

> « *It's too late to eat.* »
> ***Neith*** : « *Yes ! And then?*

No hour to eat. »

That said, Neith walked to the kitchen. She had already prepared a snack of some rosette and cheese. On the set, two glasses and a bottle of red wine.

She sat at the small kitchen table, inviting Jimmy to do the same, to sit opposite her. Jimmy obeys. Neith pushes the wine bottle toward him.

Jimmy : « *the corkscrew.* »

Neith : « *In the drawer* »

Jimmy could not believe his ears. He looked around to locate the corkscrew drawer.

Neith : « *Behind me* »
Jimmy : « *Thanks* »

Jimmy gets up and fetches the corkscrew which was well within the scope of Neith. By going behind her to reach the drawer, he noticed once again that fragrance was familiar to him. He returned to his seat, took the bottle and uncorked it.

Ceremonial as it should be to test the wine, then, filling the glasses. Absolute silence between them. Neith eats directly out of the platter, what Jimmy does not dare to do. He simply stays polite by taking a piece of cheese.

Half an hour later the snack ended. The wine bottle has suffered. Neith feels good. She invited Jimmy to return to the salon. She seems not to do cases of Jimmy's impatience to end this visit, with in sight, his night already mortgaged.

The surprise of Jimmy came to its highest level when he heard Neith telling him :

> *« Take off your shirt ... I would like to massage your shoulders ... you seem tense.»*

No sooner said Neith disappeared into her bedroom and returned with a vial of ointment with a funny look. Jimmy stays speechless and in a last effort to try to escape that night, he dared to say in an almost inaudible voice :

> *« Listen, I have to go. It's almost 1:30, I have a long way to reach my home and I have to wake up early to go to work. »*

At the indifference of Neith, he added:

« On next week I will take some days off. You can provide me all the massage you want. But for tonight, I really must go. Would you call me a taxi?»

Neith is deaf to all his supplications. She approached and began with a firm and decisive hand to unbuttoning his shirt. Again, this characteristic fragrance tickles his nostrils. Jimmy tries to remember where he knew this fragrance. His memory failed him. He does not dare ask what is this perfume. The research of the origin of this scent in his memory gradually, becomes an obsession for him.

Once out of his shirt, Neith forced him to put himself on the belly, placed both arms along his body. She opened the vial and levied a dab of this ointment, and after heating the product by rubbing her palms, she began to effectively massage the shoulders of Jimmy. Her expertise in this area is such that, Jimmy had dozed. About an hour later, Jimmy woke up with a start. He is still on the sofa, always on the belly, visibly dizzy by this massage very beneficial that he never has gotten in his life, he who is a big fan of sauna and massage. By cons, Neith is not in the dimly lit room by the light of a big scented candle.

In a final effort, Jimmy crawled out of the sofa and starts looking for to find his hostess after having calling her twice in vain. A first glance at the kitchen without success. He noticed that the second door in the living room is ajar. He heads for the door that is in fact the door of the bedroom. He approaches and discovers Neith in this dimly lit room, lying on her bed, naked body with just a piece of cloth placed discreetly on her belly. She seemed to sleep deeply. But when Jimmy took the decision to go in on tiptoe, he heard :

« You already leave me ? »

Jimmy : *« Oh yes ! I barely have time to go , get changed and to go to work. Could you call me a taxi? »*

12

Finally back home, Jimmy could not resist the urge to go to bed. He could do no more. It's past noon when he opened the eyes. He rushed to the phone to inform his boss of his "sudden" illness, almost stuttering and giving great details on a curious stomach flu occurred during the night. It was not difficult to convince him and he quietly returned to bed without suspecting that the obsession with perfume would continue to follow its way inside him.

To become an obsession for him, It was necessary that the fragrance of this odor to be truly special. Indeed, it is not one of those classical flower arrangements according to the good old customary and traditional methods of assembling of scents, flavors, assembly orchestrated by perfumer Masters, but it seems (and this is the why Jimmy noticed so fast that strange scent) that the agreement of this perfume is made on the basis of a combination of oriental components, perhaps incense (patchouli or benzoin), vanilla , a high concentration of extracts of various plants, etc .... All exhaling a strong smell of plants, producing a rather characteristic effect and delivering a particular chemical message.

Jimmy always had a good nose. He is able to capture the odors and to analyze their composition. This is a predisposition which serves him as much in the culinary field, without claim to be a "nose" and to caress the dream to be a perfume manufacturer .

The question is: why Neith wears this perfume so special? Despite his tiredness, this recurring question now haunts his mind. He wants to understand how a particular smell so characteristic, so rare can be found carried by two different people because it's indeed a smell which was familiar to him thus initially detected and noted in his immediate environment.

If the hazard induces the fortuitous nature of a phenomenon, Jimmy can not bring himself to consider as a pure coincidence what he is noticing, and that, there would be no link assumed or proven between these two realities . So indeed, it would exist a link. But which one?

For him, such a coincidence can only result of the extraordinary combination of micro links, comparable to blood vessels leading blood to the heart through the arteries.

He lost sleep. The pillow being against the bed bedside wall, Jimmy straightened to sit , the back leaning against the pillow, a bit sitting, a bit lying, and began to reflect on this mystery that can not be elucidated. He needed to determine the possible link between Neith and what he calls his "immediate environment" even if it seems to him , completely improbable.

Secondly, and proceeding by deduction, he understands that Neith has this attraction to these oriental scents. This is not surprising since Neith is a Nubian. And who says "Nubia" says (in part) "Egypt" and who says "Egypt" thinks to the perfume dedicated to deities, perfumes of which manufacturing secrets were jealously guarded by priests and gods, which allowed them to exhale an enchanting scent. It is also whispered that when the god Amun had fallen in love with a queen, he was going to visit her in the form of a king, but his divine fragrance betrayed his real identity.

Another question for the poor Jimmy's head : why another type of fragrance just hours before during his visit home and this other fragrance in the evening on her, even if she had appeared in oriental dress?

One detail seems to have marked him : the low light in Neith's apartment (in which he had seen nothing), lighting essentially based on beeswax candles recognizable by their yellow color and their embossed appearance. He remembered suddenly of the same items found in the house of his ex during the last periods before their effective separation . But very quickly, he dismissed this idea which just was a vague reminiscence.

Floriane explained to him at that time the reasons for the beeswax candles use. She said it was necessary to create an atmosphere conducive to meditation and allow higher spirits to descend into the scene to perform their beneficial actions etc .... the beeswax candles, because of their purity (no containing fragrances or dyes) are needed for these types of meditation, the electric light source being formally prohibited by the spiritualist mage because it could produce interferences .

And finally, how could it be possible to link Floriane to Neith? He clearly remembers how he met Neith. This , from a strict statistical point of view places this probability exactly to 1 against 1. 800,000 (roughly the population of Lyon and its suburbs). Therefore, his mind has quickly abandoned this assumption.

Yet, still in his mind the persistent and nagging idea that there is a link between Neith and his past. So here he is, still sitting in bed, remembering his past life : how all began, how all ended. He is not the perfect man, but he sincerely has loved Floriane. He had done everything possible to protect against herself, even against her excesses, against her naivety, against all these "vultures" who were only after her money. But she wanted to make her own experience to understand things, and find out what is the human being, according to her own words. With her, the discussion was not possible as it is impossible to talk to a person who claims not to seek the truth, because having it already, but who is looking for her "own truth" to build her own vision of life with around her (of course) all the ingredients liable to distort her judgment.

How to consider the judgment of a person who concludes several years of marriage solely because her "cosmic fiance" does not agree with her initial choice of the man she had chosen, loved and married? How to meet this simplistic vision expertly built after months of brainwashing by a spiritualist mage who obviously wished the very best for her ? Did she still have the sense of realities?

Had she the ability to feel what happiness is? How to recognize happiness if she did not bother to pause for a moment to browse the contours of this concept of happiness , and finally enjoy the benefits? How to know if we are happy, if we do not focus on one feeling at a time? ....

Jimmy has a heavy heart. Time does not erase his pain. His heart continued to bleed in secret. It is a heartbreaker for him to see Sylvia growing up in this esoteric atmosphere terribly unhealthy and destructive. He did not want to add injury to injury by attempting any action to stop this situation. The important thing is to ensure that after each second spent with Sylvia, could be a pledge when she returns to her mother, to be a little bit more armed, protected and allowing her to support this detestable climate created by the entourage of Floriane and her circle of friends.

13

First day of holidays. The first intention of Jimmy was to go to spend green holidays, to rest in the countryside , to recover energy and to spend time with his daughter. From the time he wanted to go into the Valais in Switzerland in particular, to attend the Street Arts Festival in this good city of Zion, it was the perfect opportunity to implement this project.

Jimmy has always loved the great popular festivals, mainly those organized in the street. This is one reason why he likes to vacation in Catalunya, a region where, during the summer time, the festival is permanent.

But on reflection and because remembering the promise made to

Neith about shooting for the photos album, (the famous album), he must first meet this commitment, however if Neith agrees to honor her part of promise.

So on this first day of holidays, will he take the risk of compromising his tranquility by contacting the one who ruined his sleep a night and a day of work? No, no and no ! In this case, direction towards the Park of the Golden Head, built between the Rhone and the Brotteaux district by brothers Denis and Eugène Bühler and opened in 1857. High legendary place : a treasure including among other a head of Christ gold would have been buried. Hence its name.

It was not the day of treasure hunting. Jimmy just wanted to spend some time away from his usual preoccupations, to empty his head strolling through the zoological section in particular and the rose garden to admire the wonderful creations that are each year subject to the contest for the most beautiful rose of France.

Within Floriane's garden, Jimmy had created a parterre of roses that was his pride. Several rose of this this parterre, were from private collections, bought at exorbitant prices, and valued with his true talent of landscape architecture amateur, which he had displayed in creating this mini rose garden around the the house. He was careful and devoted much time there until his ouster by the spiritualist mage. From time to time during his stay at Floriane's house, it happens to him to have a heavy heart in front of the dilapidated state of what was once his rose garden.

Lunch at the restaurant grill, resuming the promenade, ice cream break and return home. A little tired by this ballad non stop but happy with this first day of holidays. All his daily worries seem forgotten. A bath relaxing and toning, and then call to Floriane to arrange an appointment for a new day with Sylvia.

Flood of words . During five minutes, he has been informed with the latest moods of his ex. Latest fad : to tattoo a sign of recognition as a descendant of a spirit of the sea. Mandatory conditions demanded by her "cosmic begetter" to promote the advent of her future husband. The design of this sign of recognition costs a small fortune because it was the subject of a long and very "serious" study: guess initiated by who and led by who?

Small nap on the sofa. An early evening very quiet. One of those calms, harbinger of an impending storm or an eternal peace. Appreciable calm of which we do not know by what miracle or by what desolation, things will continue to go well or at the contrary to complicate and turn to disaster.

He was not to the point of asking all these metaphysical questions. It surely was neither the moment nor the opportunity for such questioning. His early evening is perfect, a week off, the prospect of a day with his beloved daughter, maybe a movie session if courage does not miss him too much, a visit to the pub "Red Lyon's", the most famous British pub ,   for listen "one night" music bands , visiting the capital of Gaul (I mean Lyon).

So,   nothing to report on the horizon during this early night which promises well. For now, priority for the napping and the good life. Jimmy spent most of his life to research (and emphasize) the softness of a shared love, a love without decline, the sweetness of a tender complicity. He needs the sweetness of himself and gentleness toward others. He likes the quiet life. Since childhood, he felt this need. But all this time spent finding tranquility, made him lose his independence in his way of looking at his relationship with others. In addition, the misfortunes that occurred in his life have permanently reshaped his character. The sweetness that was his strength, has become a real handicap in his everyday life. Despite the hardships, he never wanted to show a stern face vis-à-vis her daughter who is the greatest sweetness of his life and his greatest success. Neither the patience nor the gentleness, has helped him to overcome the resistance of Floriane. And that is the failure of his life.

14

Second day off. Rainy morning. Laborious awakening. Jimmy enjoys the privilege of still being in bed while the others are at work. He vainly tried to imagine an activity for the day ahead sullen. Truly calm : no the project . So why not just stay in bed?

Hardly had he closed the eyelids the phone rang. Jimmy looked at his alarm clock: 10:30. He wondered who could call him at this time "so early". While hoping that, it's not a problem concerning his daughter, he decided to pick up the handset, with some trepidation.

Very quickly, hearing the timbre of the voice of his interlocutor, Jimmy knew who was calling. That was Neith who wanted to know if she could go early in the afternoon for the first photo shoot.

The sublime moment of shooting approaching. Actually, Jimmy did not prepare this session and he is not more prepared himself. Is it a lack of conviction vis-à-vis the project that seems more and more surreal or just pushed by this mysterious force against which he can not fight and that in any case, will lead him to the "thing " to which it was planned?

The key word : do not be intimidated.

First act: get up, get ready, put the apartment in order. Second act: review the handling of the new camera, look for inspiration in the bathroom, invent an attitude, develop a scenario, provide a snack. All this in just three hours.

Moreover he must have a total control of the situation.

Jimmy does not feel under pressure. In ordinary life, he's a very organized perfectionist , without the bad side of perfectionists. he's not manic. But the stakes are high. He obeys something he has not a clue and Neith appears to be the centerpiece.

However, it would be illusory to think that he can consider what happens to him as something that would have been imposed by the inevitable fate. Jimmy is someone instinctive, and has never forgotten the thought of his favorite author Marcus Aurelius, namely:

« *We must live by conforming to our nature, what remains of our life, as if we already were dead, as if our life was not to exceed this moment.»*

The present moment, all the moment, only the present moment: with its advantages, disadvantages, with or without Neith, with or without shooting session.

Then, go for Neith and the photos for the "album" !

Start-up by following the plan he had imposed to himself. Noon : quick passage to the kitchen to gain strength. Back to "business," direction : the bathroom.

Jimmy remembered the astonishment of Neith by discovering his bathroom which should be classified "World

Heritage of Humanity". He froze for a long time facing the fresco. He examined in detail the situations staged by the painter who attempted to interpret several scenes of the Odyssey with as theme, the nymph Calypso on her island.

It was already happened in the past, during his long moments spent in his bathtub, to rethink of what was the story of Calypso Ulysses madly in love with Ulysses, living in the love of Ulysses. Yes but how to render this atmosphere compared to what should be ultimately, a banal setting the stage for an imaginary album ? An album is not meant to tell a story. So how to ensure that the photos may suggest this atmosphere and demonstrate at the same time the "know - how" of an amateur photographer with a certain megalomania plus, a bathroom as a photographic studio ?

Time goes quickly. Jimmy got now an idea of how things will happen. The key is to know under what mood Neith could be at her arrival. From his own experience he knows what kind of character she can be , how things can quickly cut short with her and how unpredictable she can be.

The doorbell rings . Jimmy takes a last look at his facility and opened the door.

Jimmy sees Neith for the third time and once again he finds another person. It is to wonder if nature does not return from time to time to pass a brush stroke to perfect the features of some people. Neith is resplendent. It is written somewhere :

«What is the one that appears like the dawn, who is beautiful like the moon, resplendent like the sun but terrible as an army?»

Seeing Neith, Jimmy could not prevent himself from feeling a sudden fear to see that, once again, the situation escapes him. He might want to play "George Hamilton", but for this , first, he must be credible, master of the situation and be the one to control because after all, It is indeed a performance of service and he is the customer until proven otherwise. Do not they say that the customer is the king?

Hardly had the door open, Neith launched a hello and rushed into the apartment, swiftly. Jimmy closes the door.

« *Do you have lunch ?* » asks he.

Neith :

« *Not yet, but I'll eat later. With what do we begin ? What is your plan?* »

Faced with this avalanche of questions, Jimmy tries to look good. He began to explain his scenario. While he laid out his grand theory about what should be the common thread in this session of shooting, Neith opened her big bag and began to search feverishly inside in research of something.

Jimmy's plan is anything but clear. To integrate this plan to the reality of the mural above the bathtub, he must make a transposition of the wonderful story of the Odyssey through his photos. In short, a personal interpretation of

Greek mythology in a few photos. Reading the Odyssey is already not a simple thing for the neophyte that he is. In addition, using a bathroom to restore the atmosphere of this island of the nymph Calypso, seems a totally delirious business. But Jimmy does not care about all this and wants to realize this photos session no matter the cost

    Jimmy : « *Do you have a sarong or scarf?* »
    Neith : « *Yes, I'm searching it.*»
    Jimmy : « *Ok, Go to change yourself in my room and when you will be ready, come join me in the bathroom* ».

Neith obeyed and disappeared for a time in the bedroom then reappeared at the door of the bathroom. Jimmy does not believe his eyes. Faced to him, a totally transformed person: Neith just tied around her waist a sky blue sarong . The nakedness of her chest, reveals small breasts curved, copper color with brownish nipples. A fake diamond adorns her navel. From her sarong , gush long thin legs, almost fragile. The nails of her feet are painted bright red of the same shade as the lipstick. Her hair loose, floating on her shoulders. A light make-up on her face . But her eyes are highlighted by a discreet navy blue shade , at the level of her upper and lower lashes, intensified by a pencil in the same tone. As always, lips painted bright red.

Face to Jimmy, Neith smiles, spreads her arms in cross , then swings on herself as to offer a vision of 360°.

Neith : « *OK for you ?* »

Jimmy is almost speechless. His mouth is dry. He is hot everywhere. Big urge to scratch under the arms. He regains consciousness, then with a barely audible voice:

« *Perfect ! Come in !* »

Neith enters into the bathroom hesitantly. She looked questioningly at the master of ceremonies who invited her to take the position at the edge of the tub in order to hide Calypso's image and create a visual perspective integrating her into the Odyssey panorama. Neith is both represented in three dimensions on the flat surface which is the mural, and seen from a distance, as a part of the panorama.

A final adjustment. Jimmy took a few steps back out of the bathroom for proper framing. Neith holds the right position. Then began the "grapeshot".

jimmy is like transported, multiplying the positions and view angles, making some comments like :

« **Yes ... That's it ! !!!! ....
Beautiful !!!! ..... Perfect !!! .....**»

After about a half hour of an intense photographic activity, Jimmy decreed a break. He gently placed the camera on the table alongside the old album still in its packaging, then walked into the kitchen recover the snack tray and put it on the dining table.

Neith took her place around the table. Suddenly, thunder rumbles outside: a big storm is brewing. The room dims and everything is at a standstill. Jimmy uncorked the bottle of red wine but served beforehand, a glass of water to his guest, as it is done in his country on his island. He did the same for himself.

Neith is silent. She stares at him while drinking her glass of water. Jimmy continues the implementation of the snack. In the plates, white chicken marinated in lemon juice, grilled and accompanied by a few leaves of lettuce. At his turn , he took place at the table, in front of her. She did not stop looking at him.

Suddenly she stood up and walked to the bedroom. She returned to the table, wearing a t-shirt above her sarong.

Jimmy : « *Are you cold ?* »
Neith : « *No, you're dressed ... .. I do the same like you.* »

Jimmy is a little bit confused :

« *I can remove my shirt if it suits you.* »

Neith smiles :

« *That's before you had to do it. ... .. Before I do notice it to you.* »

Jimmy gets up from his chair, takes off his shirt and sat back.

Neith takes off her t-shirt at her turn, grabbed her plate and glass, and comes beside Jimmy

« Make me a small place. »

Jimmy extracts the chair next to hers and expects to see her, to sit down. Nothing happens.

Neith :
«Everything must be explained to you? (big sigh)»

Jimmy understands less and less what happens. For him, Neith is about to go into a spin again. Once again, he expects the worst.

Jimmy : *« I do not understand »*

Exasperated to see that her host does not understand anything about anything, Neith puts the plate and glass on the table in front of Jimmy , forces Jimmy to stand up from the chair he was sitting, makes him sit down again, settling herself on his thighs, an arm around his neck, takes her glass of wine and very calmly :

« cheers !»

Jimmy is petrified. He timidly raised his glass and took a good swig. He desperately needed to drink , because, here he is at a table, half naked with on his knees, a half-naked woman and around his neck, a frail arm, warm and enveloping, forcing him to some nearby (even a certain promiscuity) with his guest. Thus , by this improvised body against body, his skin and hers are now in direct contact. Jimmy could feel the warmth of her body and the tip of her small breast , pointing on his chest. Neith does not seem to be concerned about all this and began to eat directly from her plate, and as usual with her hands. Jimmy tries to do the same, but it frankly is not easy because forced to use his left hand, the right being "requisitioned" to keep the lower back of Neith and ensure her a minimum of comfort to enjoy the snack.

Neith is increasingly sticky, imparting to her pelvis, uncoordinated movements, jerky, almost forgetting that she is sitting on the thighs of Jimmy, and not on a chair. For his part, Jimmy who is not far from the muscle cramp, continues to look good, trying vainly, not without some embarrassment to keep Neith strictly sitting on his thighs.

Occasionally, Neith slips a piece of chicken into his mouth. Jimmy has no choice but to open his beak and receive a mouthful.

At the end of what was a snack, Neith got up, picked up the plates and carried them to the kitchen and returned a while later with a plate of grapes.

Jimmy was surprised to find that all the grapes were without pips, and finely, harmoniously presented on the plate.

Neith took possession of Jimmy's thighs. Outside, a real squall causing whistles through the blinds. A time not to put a cat outside. A time to stay under the duvet.

Neith : « It's so good to be

here together. »

What to respond to a very attractive person, obviously infatuated, quite probably drunk, definitely and dangerously unpredictable, terribly sensitive to noise of raindrops on the window sill which result in a state of unparalleled excitement ? What to do against the goodness and generosity of a person who took the necessary time to eliminate grape seeds, grain by grain and feeds him by placing them gently between his lips with her mouth? How to fight against the onslaught of a creature come from nowhere and who subjugates him at the point to leave him completely defenseless? Such a similar atmosphere is obviously fatal to anyone virtuous and well balanced.

Jimmy completely succumbs . What

should have been and remain a strictly professional relationship is about to tilt dangerously. Jimmy is in great danger. He is sinking. He tries to remain stoic, even if all is happening against his will, beyond his understanding and out of reach of any resistance because Neith decided that it was the D-day . Any resistance is useless .... (whatever .....)

Neith is far from to be a obsessed with sex. However a hint of exhibitionism confers to her, this freedom characterized by her way of being : a little shocking but extremely determined. She wants Jimmy for some very special reasons (really?), And this necessarily must go through the sex channel. She is ready to satisfy this goal. Jimmy seems to correspond to this type of vigorous man she is looking for. For Neith, there is no reason to procrastinate.

Jimmy took the opportunity of a new return of his "assailant" to the kitchen to get up and get out of this confinement between his chair and the table. He takes a few steps to stretch his legs and then walked to the toilet. Moments later after using the toilet, that was his surprise to see Neith strolling integrally naked toward the bedroom, a glass of brandy in each hand.

Neith : « *You come ?* » She said just before disappearing into the room.

Jimmy imagines what will follow. He cannot prevent himself from thinking about those other old precepts , these bizarre ideas conveyed from his distant land, the land of his ancestors, which say that, all that is feminine is weakening for the buck, the warrior ... .. the semen being the strength and the life that must not be wasted ...... the woman should not show her feelings in public ... the breasts are appreciated when they are opulent..... That is considered as a sexual invitation sent by a woman when she let a man touch her breasts .... etc ... etc ...

Maybe, but Neith is a Nubian and not a Solomonic. Her small breasts has been touched by his chest. According to him, all the conditions to accept this invitation to join her in the room are not met, but the main one is that he "officially" has been invited in due form according to the code of seduction considered in his island.

Jimmy enters in turn into the bedroom. Neith is sitting on the bed, legs crossed, holding his glass of brandy. But just when he was going to grab the glass, she changed her mind, demanding him to be naked.

Very modestly, Jimmy turns, unbuttons his khaki shorts, removes with a slow movement, his shorts and underwear. Neith observes the scene, fully satisfied with this vision of these impressive buttocks from the solomon islands, firm and plump, happy in anticipation of the extraordinary power that emerges from these hips, from this solid and muscular back .

Neith : « *Your glass*»

Jimmy finally turns to face Neith. Oh

God !!! (She said) The expression of the body is sufficient in itself : Neith's "work" had peaked. That's beautiful. That's radiant. That's powerful. That's visible at a thousand miles around.

Jimmy invites Neith to get up. They are face to face, glass in hand. solemn moment in the late afternoon of the second day off. He leans forward and gently kisses her lips. Neith gives back the kiss to him by a succession of little kisses. They drink the brandy in one gulp. She puts the glass on the nightstand. He did the same. They are closer now. Their hands are free . Doing one with her. Practice the sexual act with her to achieve the perfect unity and reach the fullness of a state that is more intense than the orgasm itself, what excludes de facto any explosive orgasmic event. Sexual energies not being evacuated. They are reinjected into the body. Principle of the "Turbo" in an engine, if this comparison could be bold and no appropriate.

Jimmy has always sought to cultivate this "science" of sex to avoid sex for sex. For him, sexual pleasure is not an end in itself. The goal is to go as far as possible both in one body to energizing body and not to give up vital the energy in an uncontrolled manner in a disordered body in a full shaking.

Neith, as a wild vine, performs with her arms, her body, her legs , through undulating movements around Jimmy. The goddess Shiva would not have done better. Although his excitement was at its highest level and prisoner in this liana forest, Jimmy managed to regain control of the situation. His powerful arms are now closed on this frail and trembling body. She can not continue her "wave dance". She can not escape, so much the pressure of his arms is strong. No interest to fight . Did she want to fight? Does she said her last word?

She is desirable. She knows it. She felt no fear about a hypothetical rejection by Jimmy. She does not wonder what this relationship will become, if the fading of the sensations of early hours , would be likely to jeopardize her projects. (Ah? her project ? What project?) She knows why she's there. She knows that it is the D-day .

Suddenly, she manages to free herself from the noose, pushes Jimmy onto the bed. Then she went to the salon to get her big bag and comes back into the bedroom. She puts the bag on the ground, she crouched, began to search again within this awesome bag and pulls out a vial dyed red glass.

Neith : « *Let me do it !* »

Even before Jimmy had time to realize what is happening, here she is astride on the pelvis of her stallion, with the open vial, spraying the massage oil on his chest. She starts massaging his solar plexus in the sense of clockwise.

Jimmy : «*What are you doing to me?* »
        Neith : « *Chuuuuuuttttttt !!!!! Let me do it* »

Neith, with calm and determination, like a predator, continues to massage, gently, carefully while holding Jimmy in the bottom of the bed, and muttering in an imploring voice barely audible :

« *... Please, let him to me .... He is mine ... .. Let him to me please .... please...* »

Jimmy sank into a deep sleep. When he awoke in the middle of the night, Jimmy is alone on the bed that was in an incredible pandemonium. A real battlefield. No trace of Neith, but a strong odor reminiscent of the famous oriental fragrance. Impossible for him to remember what happened.

15

Third day off. Jimmy is ill at ease and in a very bad mood. He can not stand to have lost the thread of what happened to him the night before. In addition, he continues to smell constantly that characteristic scent on his body. This odor emanating from this massage oil of which he remembers before falling into a deep sleep. Shower after shower, aeration nonstop of the bedroom. Nothing can help. The smell is persistent. He wants to understand what happened to him late yesterday afternoon. He vaguely remembers a scene. He sees Neith again astride on his pelvis, massaging his chest. He also sees her again , getting up and going to talk to someone, half-wrapped in an almost blinding glow of species standing in the doorway. A kind of confabulation. He could not hear or understand what was being said between them. He could not move because plated mysteriously in his bed, as maintained by an invisible force to prevent him from rising. He remembers Neith, returning to place herself on him as before the sight of this "apparition". He remembers to have felt a peculiar sensation of intense heat, there was intromission followed by a sexual act of a rare violence , as if the frail body of Neith had magically, suddenly tripled in size and was considerably heavy. He still felt throughout the body, body aches as if it really had and greatly abused his athletic body. His muscles are aching. His fatigue is real and extreme. He feels emptied. He has no energy. He does not understand.

Yet throughout the day, all his attention was focused on the discovery of what happened. Gradually, things become clearer in his mind. What is sure, he has not dreamed. Neith exists. A glass of red wine , plus a glass of brandy , can not justify alone the sudden loss of consciousness. He felt good, not drunk. His excitement was at its peak. His desire to possess Neith was unparalleled. He knew that the "thing" was to take place. That filled him with happiness. What more natural to desire that person with small breasts, color copper ? What's more exciting than feeling on his skin, the contact of the intimate parts of a person who rides you in a special way ? What if all of a sudden, your strength fails and plunges you into a deep sleep? What happened between her overlap and the diving in his deep sleep?

Subjected to this intense and intolerable questioning, Jimmy continues to put his apartment in order. Removing the bed sheet to insulate all the clothes in the bag of dirty laundry and eliminate the odor left by Neith's massage oil, he was surprised to discover on the place under his pillow, a sign drawn with the oil, directly on the fabric of the mattress but, half absorbed by the fabric. He can nevertheless guess the outline of this mysterious sign that can in any way be the result of prolonged use of the mattress on which day after day, he put his head, sometimes sweaty. This can not be a coincidence. Moreover, it was not the first time he changed his sheets, and he has never seen that.

Due to his profession of graphic

designer, he perfectly knows recognize the formalism of geometric figures. By reflex and before the fabric of the mattress finishes "drinking" the oil, he searched a pen and paper to reproduce the sign seen on the matress and hides it preciously in his nightstand.

A little bit marked by this discovery, he continued his inspection : the mattress is raised and carefully inspected the bed as well. Nothing! Also the drawer of the bedside table. Nothing special. The usual mess: cream tubes, condoms, double keys, coins, ... Nothing suspicious. Direction the bathroom : no visible signs. Direction the kitchen where Neith had spent some time to empty the grapes. Like looking for a needle in a haystack. Precisely, what is he seeking ?

So, failing to make a new discovery, Jimmy went lounging in a hot bath to relax his battered body. He thinks about the photo shoot. A success from his point of view. He has not watched the pictures , but he thinks he did well. He has not rewritten the Odyssey but it was a good time for him to revisit this history. And this initiative had allowed him to escape the shame.

The memory of that photo shoot was a little lessened his concern about the rest of this day. He did not remember all the details. He keeps in a corner of his head, all steps to clarify some points of this puzzle. He also must go to the mall for large format prints of the pictures.

Back to the mall, Jimmy sit at the

table in the dining room, and he arranges the pictures on the table, the one next to the other for an overview. A detail caught his eye : Neith was wearing a pendant. A discreet pendant. Jimmy had not noticed it during the shooting session. Using a magnifying glass, he tried to detail the characteristics of this pendant. He dares not to convince himself that the shape of this pendant vaguely recalls the reproduction made from the sign sketched on the mattress. He refuses any confusion, even if the first visual observations tend to encourage him to continue along this way.

Yet , for him it is impossible to focus on one subject at a time. This accumulation of events over several weeks, these phenomena that are totally foreign to him, this person named Neith who entered his life so unexpectedly etc ... .., how could he focus on one subject at a time?

He must first of all, clarify the vision of this luminous entity that stood in the doorway and talked with Neith. He did not have a hallucination. A glass of brandy could not alter his vision. His poor brain has not stopped rehashing this. And the image of the entity turning loop in his head, the more precise the idea of a possible belonging of Neith to this category of female succubus, kind of demonic spirits whose main characteristic is to take the appearance of a attractive woman to charm men mainly while they sleep to better steal their life energy through their semen. A kind of fuel for them. Indeed, this is the second time, in lying down position and in the presence of

Neith, that he fell like by magic into a deep sleep. Then, the question is : during this period of time during which his sleep was so deep, what happened every time? Why felt he so tired the last time as if all his strength had been pumped to the point of ending up without any energy?

For being interested in the past by this kind of subject, for reasons that have nothing to do with the situation which is currently the subject of his concern, Jimmy knows that in this case, it is written that, the amorous female demon inhabits the body of a woman (usually with an amazing beauty), with who this entity would be "married" in the world of dreams. His culture does not go beyond these considerations, even though he has some predisposition (due to his origins) to believe in the paranormal.

How imagine Neith in such a posture? This frail body could it be inhabited by some unknown entity, greedy of sperm to replenish its vital energy? How else to explain why the body of Neith had suddenly weighed down considerably when she rode him? And the extreme fatigue after this? ... A thousand unanswered questions. At least, they have the merit of having been asked.

Regarding this oriental fragrance he had smelled on Neith, was known of him (no doubt): how to explain it? This question echoes in his head since his visit to Neith in Venissieux. For him, the key to this mystery will be found from the time when he can make the connection between Floriane and Neith, the time he could find the common denominator of these two people. Enter into the circle of Neith's friends, could be a first step, a good track to start. So, will he see whether or not there is an intersection to explore, namely mutual friends (Floriane / Neith) could explain the phenomenon of fragrance and deduct what danger there would be to be in a partnership with Neith in the biblical sense .

Seizing the pretext of getting news about her, Jimmy gave a phone call to Neith and proposed to go for a drink at the Red Lyon pub. Neith welcomed this invitation, as usual coldly and emotionless. No mention of what happened the night before. As if nothing had happened.

To the question : « **Did you well get**

back home last night? », the answer is invariably : « **Yes, I did** », nothing more. Not even : *« And you ? Slept well ? »*. Nothing !

Jimmy, without losing courage, trying to provoke the discussion: « *I, I think having slept like a log.* ».

Neith : « *I saw that !!! »* she said .

Jimmy : « *And you haven't told me before you go? »*

Neith : « *To do what ? »* on an almost aggressive tone.

Jimmy temporizes, then : « *To say goodbye for example. You know, it is normal to say goodbye when you leave someone.... Another example: to give you a clean towel for your shower ...»*

Neith (repentant): « *Yes I know* ».

Jimmy (a cut above) : « *Did you like yesterday?* »

Neith : « *the photo shoot ?*»

Jimmy : « *Yes the photo shoot and the rest ... .* »

Neith (playing the fatalistic woman) : « *This should eventually happen ...... And you, you've liked?*».

Jimmy : « *I think I was a bit in an irreal world .... You spoke to me, I could not answer ... .. Sorry of letting you to do all the job .... It seemed to me that you had left me for a while before returning to the attack .... I do not remember much ... .. Sorry! .... What has really happened? You literally* *have exhausted me*»

Neith (a little puzzled) : « *You mean, if we had made love?* »

Jimmy : « *Yes, among other things* »

Neith : «*Yes , we did it...* »

Jimmy : « *And how was it?* »

Neith : « *Good !* » she said tersely.

Jimmy : « *... There were condoms in my bedside table ....* »

Neith (stopping him) : «*I hate condoms*»

Jimmy : « *This could be dangerous. You do not know me, I do not know you .....* »

Neith : « *If I cannot receive your seed, what is the interest of making love with* *you?»*

Jimmy : « *You mean my sperm?* »

Neith : « *Yes I do* »

Neith : « *Do not worry, I do not want to have a baby .... Besides, I can not have a baby ... . »*

Jimmy : « *Sorry!»*

Neith « *You're welcome* »

Jimmy : « *... And do you want this to continue?»*

Neith : « *It does not depend on me* »

Jimmy : « *Ah ? ... Of who could this be dependent that we meet again?»*

Neith (increasingly enigmatic) : « *... I do not live in my body ... I have a body, no more ... I can not have a baby because, I never have gotten my* *periods ... since I was born »*

Jimmy *: « You have a beautiful body, you already had heard this compliment , a billion times »*

Neith *: «Did you hear what I just said?»* she said, dryly.

Jimmy *: « Yes Neith .... You are telling me things beyond my understanding ... Either you say it more clearly, or..... »*

Neith *: « Even if I told you all, I'm not sure you could understand ... Understand for example that from my birth I have been engaged with a water spirit ... For that, I cannot dispose of my body as I would have liked it ... For that, my nights are terrible ... For that, I cannot keep any boyfriend ... For that, all my relationships end up* *incredible disputes ... For that, any men cannot approach me ... .. Do you understand? »*

Jimmy's brain begins to bubble. This sudden and almost complete confession allows him to make a first analysis of the situation, a first approximation: water spirit on one side, spirit of the sea on the other, betrothed since birth to one side, cosmic creator of another, jealous fiance on one side, omnipresent cosmic creator of the other, etc ....

There, the similarities end (compared to Floriane) . For the rest: Floriane is a complete woman who has procreated, not Neith, Floriane is married twice during substantial periods even though her weddings ended by a divorce every time, not the least husband at the horizon for Neith, ...

Jimmy : « *Yes, in part. Is there anything to do? You touched on around you, with your friends, for example? ... You tried to negotiate with your fiancé who came from water?*»

Long and deep sigh of Neith. "FRIENDS? " She does not know what that word means. Every time she lifted the veil on her secret, the so called "FRIENDS" have cleared out the one after the other. Even the most enterprising and promising lovers, remain lovers just for a night. They could not stay with her, and they did not know why. Her life is a real emotional desert. Her loneliness is extreme and unbearable.

Moreover, Neith had not told him

everything. She could not tell him that spirit comes regularly take possession of her body when lying down. Which causes terrible pains in her joints. A big relief when finally "he" leaves her in the morning. She can then fall asleep in a deep sleep. She can not tell him that the seed of her lovers of a night, is used by the spirit to regenerate its vital energy . She cannot tell her that things may be changing to the extent that, the night before, the mind could not inhabit her as usual at the time of lovemaking because Jimmy would have inside him, something repulsive which not allowing the spirit to be in contact with his skin. Hence the discussion in the doorway of the room, the spirit's order telling her to go away from him, but in vain. That was the first time in her lifetime, she took for her own, all the fun of a successful copulation, complete and intense, hence the violence of this sexual act of which Jimmy had vaguely lived in his half-sleep. And this lasted all night, hence his extreme fatigue. It was a long time that Neith had not enjoyed such a pleasure to be with a man.

16

Fourth day off. Sylvia's special day. Home-coming planned since long dates. Excitement at its height. Permission to miss school. Booking a rental car. The more time passes since the separation from Floriane, more the need to be with his daughter, becomes increasingly obvious. Floriane's lifestyle within her friends circle, has always been a concern for him. Not because of herself, but mainly because Sylvia is exposed to the unhealthy atmosphere in which Floriane delights, since years, long before his divorce. Jimmy is very sensitive on this issue and demonstrated extreme vigilance when it comes to his daughter.

Chez Floriane, the day began to great effect. For this glorious day full of promises, a beautiful dress is needed : That is the privilege of Dad to find the activities which will match with. The week before, Sylvia and her mom had scoured the stores in the city to look for the famous dress. Each visit with her dad is the opportunity to buy a new outfit. Jimmy knows by heart the coquetry of his daughter. He is amused because he thinks of the one who will have the heavy privilege to be his son in law later. He must have the means of his policy, of course.

His relationship with Sylvia is a symbiotic relationship, sometimes making Floriane jealous . How could it be otherwise? Because of the long hours in isolation forced on the upstairs during séances, the father and daughter have come closer. They are very happy when they are together. They are very accomplices. Nothing matters when these two are together, hand in hand, strolling in parks or in the Saint Jean district. Jimmy is proud of this miscegenation that gives to her daughter a special beauty. Her face recalls in some ways the Melanesian girl, apart the expression of her stare reminiscent of her mother.

Here he is in front of the pavilion. He descends from the rented car and comes ringing at the gate. He has a key, but he does never use it. Floriane appears at the door and invites him in. Some important things to tell him.

Jimmy complied the order to get in. Inside, Sylvia chomping at the bit and ran welcome her dear papa.

« OH ! How beautiful you are !!!!»

exclaimed Jimmy on seeing her daughter in her new dress. A chiffon dress, pearl gray, Pan collar with a pale pink edging. A pair of black varnished ballerina showing her little white socks with silver highlights like Michael Jackson. Relaxed hair (miss does not like when her hair buckle), tied with a silk gray knot . A small handbag, gift from her father at her last birthday.

Jimmy is on his knees to greet his little girl adored that rushes madly in his arms. They are clamped against each other for a long time until that :

« Can I talk to you ? »

Floriane has things to say.

Jimmy : « *That cannot wait until tonight?* »
Floriane : « *OK OK !!!!!* »

© *Nathanaël AMAH , 2016*   *NATHAM Collection*

Jimmy does not want to let her to start unpacking her life. They will have for the day. He prefers to cut short, waiting the night, as he is invited to share dinner as usual to prolong the day spent with her daughter. Generally this happens like that , by agreement with Floriane. Sometimes, she has dinner at Jimmy's apartment , when she goes to pick up Sylvia .

Here they are installed in the car.

Jimmy : « *What do you want to do my dear?* »
Sylvia : « *What you want Dad.* »

Jimmy wants to do as always, a maximum of things with his daughter. Direction central Lyon. First stage of the day : the shoping. Jimmy does not like to spend time in stores, but for his daughter, this exercise becomes bearable provided that it does not last too long. An hour to walk through the shops, Sylvia revealing herself to be a real woman in miniature in what she may have in her attitudes of hesitation and reversal in the choice of clothing. Jimmy looks good. He does not want to rush her daughter. He is to her disposal. Second step : a small snack while waiting for lunch. A cup of hot chocolate in a tearoom in Republic Street.

Jimmy : « *Are you ok ?* »
Sylvia : « *Yes Dad* »
Jimmy : « *At school too ? … It's almost the holidays ?* »
Sylvia : « *Yes Dad.* »

Sylvia finished drinking her cup of chocolate while licking her lips. Jimmy noticed the laconic answers of his daughter to his questions. Generally, Sylvia is much more talkative. But he expects that his daughter decides herself to talk to him if really there is something to know. He has great confidence in his daughter. They take their time in this coffee shop, Jimmy took the opportunity to swallow two or three financial and rebuild his stock of various cakes, and did not forget the beggars, delicious chewable in the evening when watching television.

He told her a little about his early week off, especially his trip in the park La Tête d'Or. Sylvia knows this park very well, having been there so many times. They also discuss about the next summer holidays , during the month where he will have full custody of his daughter. Sylvia who likes the surprises, does not express a precise choice, outside the range of proposals made by her father. What is certain, she loves to fly, no matter where the plane takes her. She told her father the choice of her mother for the next holiday : they will go somewhere in Asia. She does not remember much of the country name, but whatever...

Jimmy was not returned to his native island for a long time. He had planned to make this trip with his family but Youssoufou had decided otherwise.

It is a painful memory for him when he remembers a time when everything was perfect within his family, period where everything was possible. He has in him a real resentment for Floriane's entourage. Sometimes he feels guilty by thinking he could have avoided this tragic end of her marriage, pointing to firmer, more master within his couple. After all, how it can be than, an insignificant individual can come with impunity to take the power in his home and divert his wife, even if it is established that the said wife was a woman under influence? He bitterly regrets.

That's why he holds his daughter as the apple of his eye. He always has an eye on her, ready to intervene in any situation. Sylvia knows that. She knows that her father watching over her. This helps her a lot even if she is not really unhappy with her mother.

During the time her father lived at home, she acquired the reflex to isolate herself when "Friends" of her mother landed in the living room and her mother was transfigured, having only eyes, attention and respect for her friends. Ah the good FRIENDS !!!!! The dear FRIENDS !!!!!

A final visit at the "pee room" then here they are in the street, a few steps in the center of Lyon, while going towards the parking to store the packets in the car before lunch.

12:30. Restaurant "NORTH" somewhere in the center. Sylvia is very proud to be in this place where the cuisine is inspired by a famous chef and multi starred. Her father had briefed her about the story of this restaurant. Her dress is perfect for the occasion. Jimmy has always loved the high places of the gastronomy of Lyon.

And it is without hesitation that, he shares this passion with her daughter, who despite her young age, seems to enjoy the pleasure of eating good food and patronize the good tables with her dear papa.

It was an uneventful lunch. No much exchange between them. Then, digestive walk hand in hand. Next surprise? Visit to a museum dedicated to silk. Sylvia has always wanted to understand the job of her father. She has in her wardrobe a collection of silk scarves offered by her father. Some of her scarves are done by her father. She keeps them preciously , although occasionally she finds them around the neck of her mother. Just a borrowing between girls.

During the visit in the museum, she

learned how is born a silk scarf. She had the right to choose in the gallery of the museum sales, a scarf given by her father to complete her collection.

At the end of the visit, another surprise awaits : a Guignol show in the park la Tête d'Or. Sylvia is right audience. The new show   pleases her a lot. It was fun. She seems happy.

In order not to tire her too much, because there is school the next day, Jimmy offers to go get some rest before dinner. Sylvia immediately accepted .

But in moving towards the park exit, Sylvia suddenly freezes and holds strongly the hand of his father. She cannot advance anymore. Jimmy noticed the attitude of his daughter and immediately asks :

« *What's the matter ? Tell me, what is it?* »

Sylvia is unable to speak. She let go the hand of her father and grabbed his leg. Jimmy managed to kneel at its height to take her in his arms and reassure her. Sylvia pushes the face in her father's neck. Now, Jimmy is really worried.

« *What happens   honey? Sylvia, Sylvia, look at me, tell me what's wrong? talk to me .....*»

In front of the silence and awe of his daughter, Jimmy eventually take her in his arms. His neck is enclosed in the small arms of his daughter who keeps her face hidden. He takes the way, in a hurry to exit the park through the crowd of mothers and children who attended the Guignol show .

Suddenly, in the opposite crowd of visitors entering the park, Jimmy in turn freezes. Face to him, Neith, all dressed in white from head to foot : sari, scarf and white ballerinas.

Jimmy cannot believe in coincidence. Neith goes to him.

Neith : « *Good evening!»*
Neith : « *Good evening Miss !»*

Jimmy gazed her in the eye. Sylvia does not move from her position, the face still buried in her father's neck.

Jimmy : « *Good evening !»*
Neith : « *You're out? »*

Jimmy : « Yes we do, and you, what are you doing here!»
Neith : « I take a walk . You introduce me your daughter?»

At this request, Sylvia expresses her disagreement by increasing a little more pressure around her father's neck. Jimmy understands the message.

Jimmy :   «My daughter is tired. We were on our way back home »
Neith : « What is her name? »
Jimmy : « Sylvia .»
Neith : « Sylvia ? It is the name of the daughter of one of my friends in Caluire »

Jimmy falls from above. Floriane lives in Caluire.

Jimmy : « I have to go . See you !»

Neith : « See you !»

Neith has not seen the face of Sylvia. Jimmy did everything to not expose his daughter. After a few steps toward the park exit :

Sylvia : « She left ? »
Jimmy : « Who are you talking about ? »
Sylvia : « Danae»
Jimmy : « Who ?»
Sylvia : « The woman who spoke with you »
Jimmy : « Her name is Danae? Are you sure ? Do you know her ? Have you already seen her?»

He asks while continuing to walk with a firm step, with Sylvia clinging to his neck.

Sylvia : « Yes, she sometimes comes home. She's a mom friend.»

Sylvia : « I don't like her at all. She scares me»

Jimmy : « Why she scares you?»

Sylvia : « She sometimes comes into my bedroom when I sleep »

Jimmy : « My Goodness !! She comes to do what in your bedroom? Your mom knows this ?»

Sylvia : « No»

Jimmy : « She does what when she comes into your bedroom?»

Jimmy continues walking to his car.

Sylvia : « I see her in front of my bed with a man »

Jimmy : « WHAT ?»

Jimmy came near to the rental car. He opens the door and Sylvia moved to the back and fastened her belt. He sits down a moment to the back by her side to comfort her. He takes her by the hand. He remains silent for a moment.

Jimmy : *« Who's this man who comes with her in your bedroom?»*

Sylvia takes a desolate and distraught face , and she turns her head to her father.

Sylvia : *« I do not know Dad ...... He shines »*
Jimmy : *« He shines ? What do you want to say honey?»*
Sylvia : *« ... It is as if he is surrounded by light. He shines .... I do not know how to tell you.»*
Jimmy : *« Did you tell mom? »*
Sylvia : *« Yes dad»*

Jimmy : « *She did what when you told her?* »
Sylvia : « *Nothing.* »

Sylvia burst into tears. Jimmy's throat tightened.. He tries to calm and comfort his daughter.

Sensing his daughter in danger, Jimmy feels anger rising in him. What to do ? Thousand ideas come to mind. But how to deal with this problem that puts her only child in danger? And if at least he knew at what real danger his daughter is exposed by living under the roof of her mother? How to stop this? Take the problem upstream by doing everything possible to remove his daughter from this toxic environment, or downstream, ie, to ensure that these phenomena do not continue. In any case, he was decided to act immediately, without wasting a minute. To do otherwise would be a failure to assist a person in danger. He can no longer endure this situation which turns into a nightmare. He will do everything to save her daughter. She has become a top priority.

17

Arrival at Floriane. Jimmy led his daughter to the door and back to retrieve packages.

Floriane welcomes them at the door. A few minutes ago she was in the kitchen preparing dinner. As always, Jimmy continues his moment with her daughter by sharing dinner.

Until now, it was to extend his one-on-one with his daughter. From today, he assigned to himself, a new mission : get his daughter out of the clutches of her mother and from this toxic environment.

While Sylvia is up to her bedroom to change and bathe, Jimmy joined

Floriane who is cooking. She serves him a glass of his favorite whiskey. Jimmy grabbed the glass and observed it for a while. No troubles elements suspended in his whiskey. He hesitates to raise the glass to his lips. Floriane has noticed the attitude of his ex.

Floriane : *« Why don't you drink your whiskey? You're afraid I poisoned you?»*
Jimmy : *« Who is Danae?»*

Floriane jumps.

Floriane : *« From where you know this person?»*

Jimmy remains undeterred. Floriane recognizes this cold anger that characterizes him and of which he has the secret, which may herald an earthquake.

Jimmy : « Who is Danae? »
Floriane : « She is a friend »

Jimmy drops the glass of whiskey on the table without drinking it, leaves the kitchen and joined his daughter in her bedroom. Stayed in the kitchen at the work plan, Floriane is lost. She can not believe that Jimmy knows the existence of Danae. So far, Jimmy had never been interested by the active members of her circle of friends in the framework of her paranormal acitivities. So why, suddenly, Danae is at the center of his concerns?

Jimmy goes down with his daughter for dinner. He installs her and sits down next to her. This is not usual. In principle, it is sitting in front of his daughter. Floriane has noticed the change , once again, but does not react to this situation. For now, she seems concerned about the issue of her ex about Danae , but she said nothing.

Dinner was without incident. Jimmy must create a soothed atmosphere and peaceful around his daughter, in default of her mother. Surprisingly Floriane who ordinarily is very talkative has almost nothing to say. She had announced her ex, her desire to tell him important things. But that was before learning that her ex knows the existence of Danae.

End of dinner. An additional half hour with his daughter before taking leave. Sylvia seems appeased. She never doubted about the support and protection of her father. She knows that whatever happens, her father will always be there to defend her and to protect her.

Jimmy embraces one last time his daughter, covering her in the bed and goes down to the ground floor.

Floriane is waiting down the steps. Obviously she waits that the storm breaks. But Jimmy simply says goodbye and crossed the doorstep. Floriane cannot believe. For her, knowing her ex, his silence does not bode well for her. She is waiting for what will follow.

Arrived at home, big surprise : a word of Neith slipped under the door.

« *Good evening, I went to see you . Neith .*»

Nothing more. Terse message that put him in a monster rage . She loses nothing by waiting. But first, priority to a bath. He needs it. His mind was scalded following revelations of his daughter. He bubbles inside. He must know what is happening around his daughter.

Always with his rental car, Jimmy back on the road towards Venissieux. The same old ascensur winded. Floor 8. Before the door of Neith. He does not ring, he drummed with his fist emphatically. He takes a look at his watch. 22:30. The door opens . Neith appears.

Jimmy : « *Good evening Danae*»

Neith smiles. She doesn't seem surprised to hear to be called "Danae".

Neith : « *Good evening Jimmy. Come in !*»

Jimmy followed suit and entered the apartment.

Neith : « *You had dinner? I prepare something for you?* »
Jimmy : « *No, thanks Miss Danae*»
Neith : « *Stop with that !!!!*»
Jimmy : « *Stop with what ? Stop calling you Danae ? Stop thinking that you haunt the nights of my daughter? I continue ?* »

In front of this unpacking, Neith disappears into the kitchen and returned moments later with a bottle of red wine and two glasses.

Jimmy : « You do not forget anything? Where is your anesthetic vial? »

Neith does not disassemble. She puts the glasses on the table next to the bottle of wine.

Neith : « You do the service? »

Jimmy remains adamant. He camped near the table with his hands in his pockets. He waits for answers that do not come. He is impatient. Neith is quiet. Very calm. She grabbed the bottle and corkscrew. She approaches him and hands him the bottle.

Neith : « Please!»

After a moment of hesitation, Jimmy deigns to remove the hands from his pockets and agrees to open the bottle of wine. He does the service and puts his hands in his pockets.

Jimmy : « And then? »
Neith : « Cheers ! »

Jimmy agrees to toast.

Jimmy : « It's coming ? I do not have all night »
Neith : « OK ! What do you want to know ? »
Jimmy : « Eveything. I want to know why my daughter is in danger in her own house. »
Neith : « Sylvia is not in danger. With me, (I mean , thanks to me) she is no longer in danger »
Jimmy : « You are laughing at me ? »

Neith : « I'm not making fun of you. I tell you the truth. »

Jimmy : « Start by telling me what is your name»

Neith : « Neith as you know it. It's my name. Trust me »

Jimmy : « Danae : your stage name? Your actress name ?

Neith smiles.

Neith : « I am not an actress»

Neith : « Danae , is like Cymbia. »

Jimmy : « Cymbia ?»

Neith : «   The baptismal name of Floriane »

Jimmy :   « How do you know my ex wife? What is the baptismal name? What are you talking about ?»

Neith : « We belong to the same prayer group. It's a coincidence if we met you and me. A real coincidence.

Believe me. .... Some events are beyond us. We cannot always explain everything, rationally.»

Jimmy *: « What does my daughter have to do with all this ?»*

Neith *: « Nothing . Absolutely nothing.»*

Jimmy *: « So why you come to haunt her nights? I will not tell you twice, let her in peace ... »*

Neith *: « It's not so easy»*

Jimmy *: « What do you mean ? »*

Neith *: « It's not so easy because Floriane is her mother and she lives with her mother. until she will be in this environment .... »*

Jimmy understands the meaning of her insinuation . She confirmed that the house of Floriane became toxic to his daughter. All satanic rituals that take place are enough to pervert the atmosphere in this place. He regrets not having done everything possible to get sole custody of his daughter. At the time, he did not want to add stress to the stress. He tried to keep a watchful eye on the education of his daughter. He was not able to measure the consequences of these repeated rituals that take place in this house. At least until today. What to do ? Initiate proceedings to obtain sole custody of his daughter alleging the sectarian abuses of his ex? Having a frank and serious discussion with his ex to explain the ravages of these rituals that take place in the house, even if she is under the influence of that bastard of Youssoufou? taking the advantage of his guard this summer to return in his country and never come back? Kill Youssoufou ?

Jimmy : « What do you mean?»

Neith : «   I think there is a way to escape to all that. But I do not know if I have the right to talk to you as I do now. I did not want to risk my life for nothing.»

Jimmy : « What are you talking about ? You come back to haunt the nights of my daughter and it's you who should be in danger? Are you kidding ? Why you do not talk to me frankly? Geez, of what are you afraid?»

Neith : «   Do you remember what I told you? »

Jimmy : « You mean the lamppost?   »

Neith : « Do not talk like that. It is a powerful entity. You should be prudent.»

Jimmy : « You told me that I pushed him away. Isn't it ? »

Neith : « Yes, and that's because of

this that Sylvia was able to escape. She is lucky. »

Jimmy : « *Why ?* »

Neith : « *Your blood flows through her veins. You have forwarded the "repulsive" to your daughter.* »

Jimmy : « *Keep going!* »

Neith : « *I do not know if I can tell you .... You put me in danger by asking me all these questions.* »

Jimmy : « *I must know ! You understand that I have to save my daughter?* »

Neith : « *Ok . You remember that I was chosen from my birth ... It's the same for your daughter, but her body is uninhabitable because of the repulsive .... this does not prevent the entity from always prowling around around her . Nothing can make him to give up . At least for now.* »

Jimmy : « *What should I do ? What*

do you recommend ? »

Before explaining what Jimmy could do to save his daughter, Neith loses consciousness. She collapses and is found on land. Jimmy rushes. She's still breathing, but not moving. Her eyes are closed. Her body seems taut and her temperature is very high. Jimmy, do not know what to do. He pats her cheeks, without result. He rushes into the bathroom and came back with a wet towel that he passes on her face. Nothing helps. Then he took his mobile and dialed the emergency number. But before he start talking :

Neith : *« It's ok ! It's ok ! »*
Jimmy : *« It's ok ? »*
Neith : *« Go home ! »*

© *Nathanaël AMAH , 2016   NATHAM Collection*

18

Like an automaton, Jimmy came to his apartment in the old Saint-Jean district, without knowing how he achieved to return at home after his eventful departure from Venissieux. His anger has not subsided. Moreover, while he was near the end, the malaise of Neith has questioned everything.. What to do with the pieces of information obtained? A glass of brandy and then to bed.

The next day, the fifth day off, Jimmy can not resist the urge to return to Venissieux.

The usual ritual: the old elevator winded, stopping on the floor #8, the door of Neith. He rings once. He rings

twice. He rings three times. At the
moment he is about to scribble a
message on a piece of paper and slide
it under Neith's door, the neighbour's
door opens. An old man goes out and
asks :

The old man : « *Who are you ? Are
you a member of her family* »
Jimmy : « *No , Just a friend.* »
The old man : « *She was so kind...*»
Jimmy : « *You know where she is?* »
The old man : « *You're not aware
of?* »
Jimmy : « *Know what?* »
The old man : « *She was found dead
in her apartment in the night* »
Jimmy : « *Dead ? What happened?*»
The old man : « *On returning home,
the neighbor of the   door in front of
hers, noticed that the door of this
person was wide open. And casting a*

glance inside, he discovered her lifeless. She was lying on the floor .....»

Jimmy is speechless. then:

« Good bye, sir ... . »

Once again winded lift. Ground floor. The street. The car .... Could not get in the car. He cannot start. He is stunned. He tries to pull himself together. He thinks about his last interview with Neith. Oh shit : he drank wine. He did not want . His glass remained on the table. His fingerprints. Big panic. Spontaneous visit to the police? .....

Armed with courage, he took the direction of Caluire. He needs to see his daughter urgently. He sounds insistently at the villa. The maid comes to open the door. Floriane still is sleeping. After a long night of spiritualism, she was exhausted. She must wake up. She must . The maid goes upstairs to wake her . Where is Sylvia? Ah yes, it's a school day. Yes ! He slumps into a armchair. Moments later, Floriane goes down, surprised to see him there in her living room.

Jimmy : *« She is dead ! »*
Floriane : *« Who is dead ? »*
Jimmy : *« Neith . »*
Floriane : *« Who ? »*
Jimmy : *« Danae »*
Floriane : *« What ? How do you know that ? »*

Very quietly, very methodically, Jimmy told her the whole story from start to finish without skipping any details.

© *Nathanaël AMAH , 2016*　　*NATHAM Collection*

Hardly as had he finished telling the whole story that the phone rang. It is the school which warns that Sylvia felt unwell and the emergency staff is on site. Parents are expected.

Floriane goes up   four at stairs to get changed and down at full speed. The rental car is parked in front of the villa.

 In front of the school, the emergency ambulance . Inside, Sylvia receives first aids pending the arrival of the parents. The medical staff explains the situation : at the beginning, a slight nosebleed treated by the teacher. Then fainting. And now in a state close to coma.

Floriane is installed in the ambulance which taking the direction of the university hospital centre of Lyon.

Jimmy follows in his rental car. University hospital centre of Lyon : admission unity . Floriane answers to the questions of the doctor to explain the traces on her daughter's body. She cannot explain the origin of these traces, neither Jimmy . Reporting to the police for an investigation into a suspected abuse. They are summoned, interrogated and released. The traces originate neither from beatings nor from any allergic manifestation. Back to University Hospital.

In the waiting room, Jimmy overwhelms her ex and threatens to reveal her occult practices to the police and to claim sole custody of his daughter, if she does not take binding commitment to put an end to these satanic practices .

Jimmy cannot prevent himself from making the connection between what happened to Neith and his daughter. He focuses on the pieces of information collected from Neith. But put end to end, these pieces of information, do not lead him anywhere. Neith has not had time to reveal the solution to save and protect his daughter. He is living a nightmare.

An idea made its way into his mind. Neith had several times mentioned the presence of a "repulsive" that held in check this powerful spirit. So, insofar as his blood flows in the veins of his daughter, and that the body of Sylvia is uninhabitable but not unattainable, he should find a fast and efficient way to make this unattainable body, once and for all.. But how to do it ? He has to find it , especially as the numerous

185   The NUBIAN   (The mysterious NEITH)

examinations of Sylvia, do not reveal no abnormality organic type or any functional dysfunction.

In his native island, the men were leaving for several days, to go fishing in the high seas. But before leaving, they always left to mothers, a garment worn by them, during twenty-four hours. This garment was carefully kept in a safe place. And if necessary, (fever or other malaise and before going to the hospital), the sick child must be covered by clothing worn by the father. And, generally, this served to help to cover health (it seems) . This is a widespread practice in the island.

OK, OK ! But Jimmy has a rational mind. He cannot explain how the printed body magnetic flows in a garment can help to treat a fever. He cannot explain it, but why not? On the other hand, Sylvia is not feverish. She is in a light coma. And he doesn't want than a charlatan touches his daughter.

He gets up and goes to the room of his daughter. Floriane is at the bedside of her daughter. Without a word, he takes off his shirt, then his undershirt. He puts again his shirt. Floriane does not understand what is happening. He carefully folds his undershirt (worn for only a few hours), and deposits it on the chest of his still unconscious girl (directly on her skin). He then grabs her left hand, and firmly holds it in his big hands and focuses on her.

He remains that way for several minutes under the skeptical gaze of Floriane. He finally releases the hand of his daughter, gently deposited it on the bed (to avoid to disturb the infusion in place in her arm since her hospitalization), takes the other hand, and do the same operation with the same delicacy.

It is a touching spectacle featuring a desperate father trying to instill life to his only daughter, through his hands, these ridiculous hands at the service of a God he does not know , and with who he has not often been in contact. Surreal image of a man immersed in a silent and intense prayer, pleading, begging. But, with who he is in communion? Always the same God who has deserted his home to give way to the devil? Floriane did not know him under this aspect. She is discovering him. She is impressed. Her heart is pounding. She would have liked to join him in the rescue operation, to add her own vital energy. But she did not dare touching him. She is overwhelmed by the emotion created by the vision of her ex, ready to give his own life for his only daughter to recover her life . It seems that faith can move mountains. But does one need to be a believer when the truth is so obvious, when the will contradicts the impossible? His concentration is so great that he seems almost in a trance.

She gets up and approaches her ex. Her eyes are close to tears. She can measure the love of Jimmy for his daughter. She feels deep pain of having letting go this man so kind, so loving, so caring, good father, who fights for the survival of his daughter.

19

Past noon. Jimmy and Floriane are sitting on either side of the bed, staring at their daughter. The nurse on duty offers them a meal tray. They decline the offer. They are not hungry. Sylvia is in stable condition but still unconscious. For now, there 's nothing to do. Just wait . The head doctor will start his visits in the afternoon. They will know more.

Quick visit of the chief doctor. Nothing new . They must wait . Here they plunged back into their respective dumbness and despair. Tme goes by slowly. It is long to wait , even if everyone is willing to spend the entire life in the hospital, if it helps Sylvia.

Floriane feels the need to take a shower. Jimmy passes her the keys of the rental car. He remains alone with his daughter. He has a tired face. He is nervously exhausted. He is on the verge of a nervous breakdown. He gets up and walks to the bedroom window. He gazes the sky for a while , then turns to get a support against the window, eyes directed towards Sylvia.

Is it an optical illusion? He seems to have seen the hand of his daughter moving. He rushes to the bed and looks carefully. Yes, the hand moves. So he gently takes the hand in his. He must continue. He focus again and remains so for minutes. Now it is clear : Sylvia actually moves her hand.

Jimmy : « *Sylvia !* »
Jimmy : « *Sylvia my sweet baby, it's*

Dad »

Moments later, without knowing how, without knowing why, Sylvia opened her eyes, a little surprised to see her dad beside her. She was at school before her malaise. She remained in this class with the teacher who came to treat her bleeding nose. She only remembers that.

Jimmy activates the nurse call . The nurse on duty arrived moments later. She has seen the evolution of the state of the patient Sylvia, and calls the chief doctor. Rechecking of basic constants. The verdict is clear: yes the patient is out of her coma. Jimmy weeps for joy. Sylvia must stay a few days under observation. Jimmy can breathe now.

Joy short-lived . The concern for the privacy of his daughter surfaced again . How to protect his daughter? He does not know why her daughter is out of the coma. He did not know if that's the Melanesian protocol implemented which helped extricate his daughter from the clutches of the devil. But what is absolutely certain, is his determination to stop the satanic practices of his ex.

Curiously, at her arrival at the villa, Floriane spent over an hour on the phone with Youssoufou, to signify to him that she ends the occult practices and that is a final decision. Youssoufou tried to dissuade her, but to no avail. She has been scalded by the sudden death of Danae and the malaise of her daughter. She became again suddenly lucid and wants to regain the control of her life. Now, nothing is more precious than the life of her daughter, nothing can divert her from her objective to change things around.

Back to the hospital, she learned the good news. She does not know how to announce her decision to Jimmy. She does not dare telling him that things have changed in her life and around her. She knows she has lost all credibility vis-à-vis him and it will be difficult to regain his confidence.

End of visiting hours. It's time to go home. Jimmy accompanies his ex at the villa.
But when leaving the vehicle :

Floriane : « *Jimmy, come back home. Please !* »

END

© *Nathanaël AMAH , 2016*   *NATHAM Collection*

Bibliography

By the same author

NATHANAËL AMAH

(NATHAM Collection)

- HARCELEMENT (Le moment où nous obetenons ce que nous voulons le plus) (2016)

- HARASSMENT (The moment we get what we want the most) (2016)

- ACOSO (El momento en que conseguimos lo que queremos mas) (2016)

- NEITH (La mystérieuse Nubienne) (2016)

Editor : BoD-Books on Demand, 12/14 rond point des Champs Élysées, 75008 Paris, France
Impression : BoD-Books on Demand, Norderstedt, Allemagne
ISBN   :   978-2-322-09538-4
Legal Deposit :   June, 2016

196   The NUBIAN   (The mysterious NEITH)